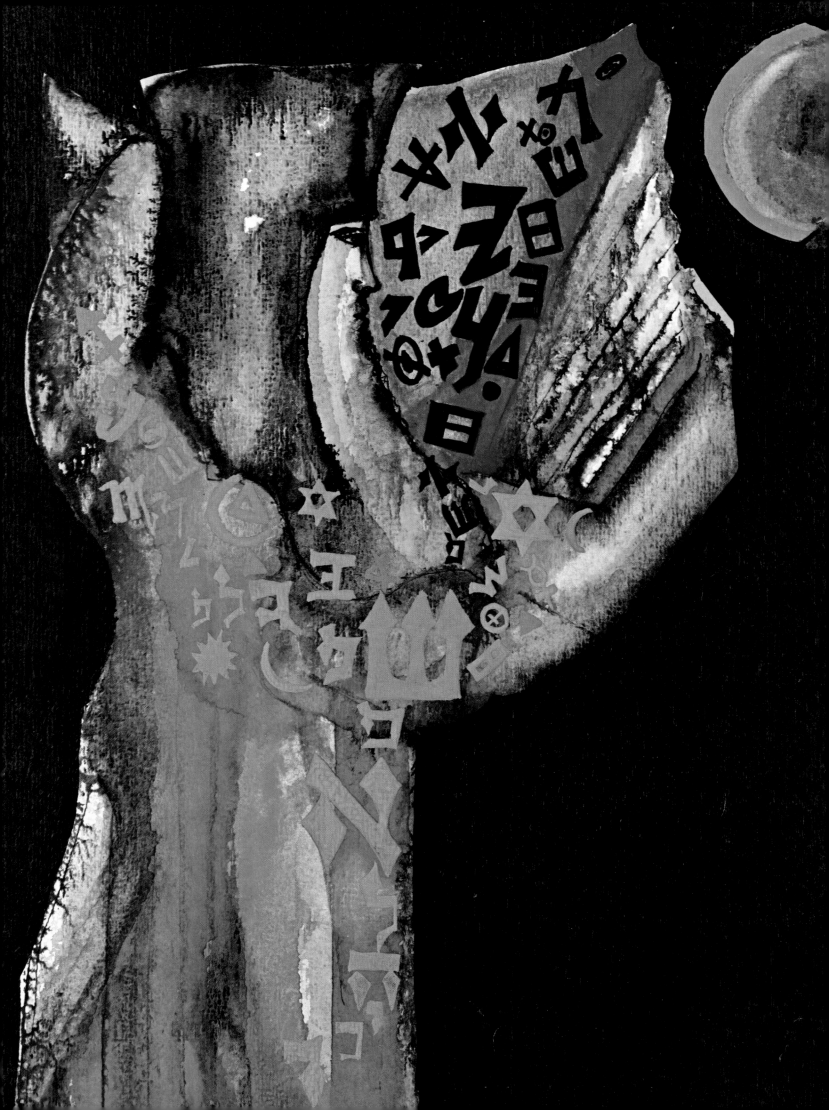

THE GOLEM

A Jewish Legend

Beverly Brodsky McDermott

J. B. Lippincott Company   Philadelphia and New York

For my mother

The quotation from *Ten Rungs* by Martin Buber is copyright © 1947 by Schocken Books Inc. and is reprinted by permission of Schocken Books Inc.

U.S. Library of Congress Cataloging in Publication Data
McDermott, Beverly Brodsky.   The Golem: a Jewish legend.
1. Judah Löw ben Bezaleel, d. 1609 — Juvenile literature. 2. Golem — Juvenile literature. I. Title.
BM755.J8M28   398.2'2   75-29136   ISBN-0-397-31674-7

About the Author-Illustrator: Beverly Brodsky McDermott was born in Brooklyn and graduated from Brooklyn College with a bachelor of arts degree. In addition to her work as an illustrator, she is a painter. Many of her paintings are color-field abstractions in oil on canvas. She lives with her husband, artist Gerald McDermott, in the Hudson River Valley.

About the Book: While living in the south of France, Ms. McDermott saw the German film *The Golem*, made in the 1920s, and was inspired to do the story as a picture book. Her research and its development took almost two years, during which she studied the symbols of the Hebrew alphabet and their corresponding magical qualities according to the Jewish mystics — the Cabbalists. About the actual work on the paintings, Ms. McDermott says, "As I explored the mysteries of the Golem an evolution took place. At first, he resembled something human. Then he was transformed. His textured body became a powerful presence lurking in dark corners, spilling out of my paintings. In the end he shatters into pieces of clay-color and returns to the earth. All that remains is the symbol of silence." The illustrations are executed in gouache, watercolor, dye, and ink on watercolor paper.

Bibliography
Bloch, Chayim. *The Golem: Mystical Tales from the Ghetto of Prague.* Translated by Harry Schneiderman. Blauvelt, N.Y.: Rudolf Steiner Publications, 1972.
Ish-Kishor, Sulamith. *A Boy of Old Prague.* New York: Pantheon Books, 1963.
———. *The Master of Miracle: A New Novel of the Golem.* New York: Harper & Row, 1971.
Meyrink, Gustav. *The Golem.* Translated by Madge Pemberton. Prague and San Francisco: Mudra, 1972.
Nahmad, H. M., comp. *A Portion in Paradise and Other Jewish Folktales.* New York: Viking Press, 1970.
Ponce, Charles. *Kabbalah: An Introduction and Illumination for the World Today.* New York: Quick Fox, 1973.
Rubens, A. Alfred. *A History of the Jewish Costume.* New York: Crown, 1973.
Scholem, Gershom. *On the Kabbalah and Its Symbolism.* New York: Schocken Books, 1965.
Trachtenberg, Joshua. *Jewish Magic and Superstition: A Study in Folk Religion.* New York: Atheneum, 1970.

The origin of the world is dust, and man
has been placed in it that he may raise the
dust to spirit. But his end is dust and time
and again it is the end where he fails, and
everything crumbles into dust.

Martin Buber,
Ten Rungs: Hasidic Sayings

March winds moaned while the people of Prague slept. Doors and shutters were fastened against the night and gates that kept the Jews in their ghetto were locked tightly.

Inside the thick walls lived the beloved Rabbi Yehuda Lev ben Bezalel. He was pious and wise, a learned man. Every day he studied the holy books and prayed with his people. It was said that he could perform miracles.

One evening Rabbi Lev heard a mysterious voice. He told his wife, Rivka, "In my dream people accused us of baking our matzos with the blood of Christian children. An angry mob attacked the ghetto and killed our people."

Rivka's face grew white with fear. She had hoped this year would bring a happy Passover festival. "Surely we are safe," she protested. "There has been no trouble for the Jews of Prague for a long time."

But Rabbi Lev was convinced that the dream was a sign. "I will mold a clay man to protect us."

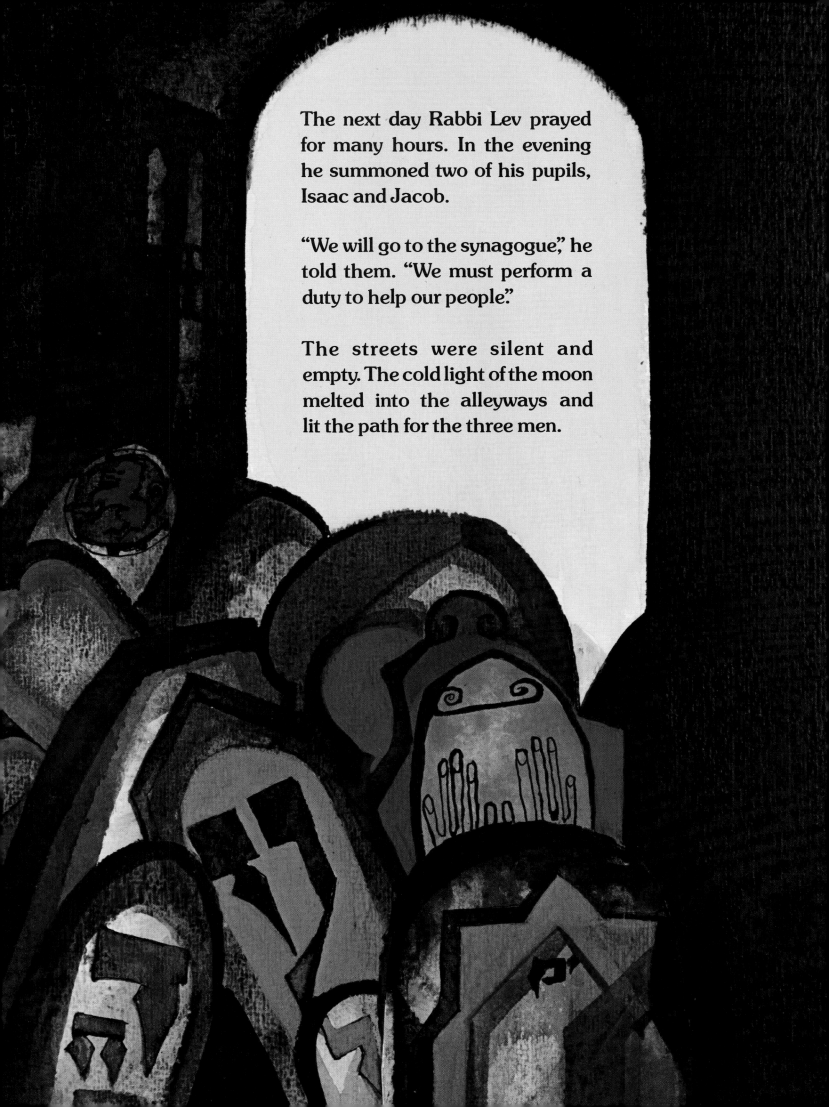

The next day Rabbi Lev prayed for many hours. In the evening he summoned two of his pupils, Isaac and Jacob.

"We will go to the synagogue," he told them. "We must perform a duty to help our people."

The streets were silent and empty. The cold light of the moon melted into the alleyways and lit the path for the three men.

They climbed the stairs that led to the attic.

There, under ancient prayer books, lay a shapeless lump of clay.

Rabbi Lev spoke calmly to his pupils. "We must use our magic to raise the Golem," he said. "I have been commanded by God."

They circled the lump of clay and chanted the secret names with which heaven and earth were created.

Rabbi Lev then molded the clay.

Suddenly, orange flames glowed and scorched the ceiling. Water flowed and extinguished the fire. Steam rose and fogged the windows.

"Look," cried Isaac. "A man is made!"

"Oh," said Jacob. "He sprouts hair and nails. He opens his mouth but cannot speak."

"Yes," said Rabbi Lev. "I can create the likeness of a man, but only God can give the gift of speech. The Golem will remain mute."

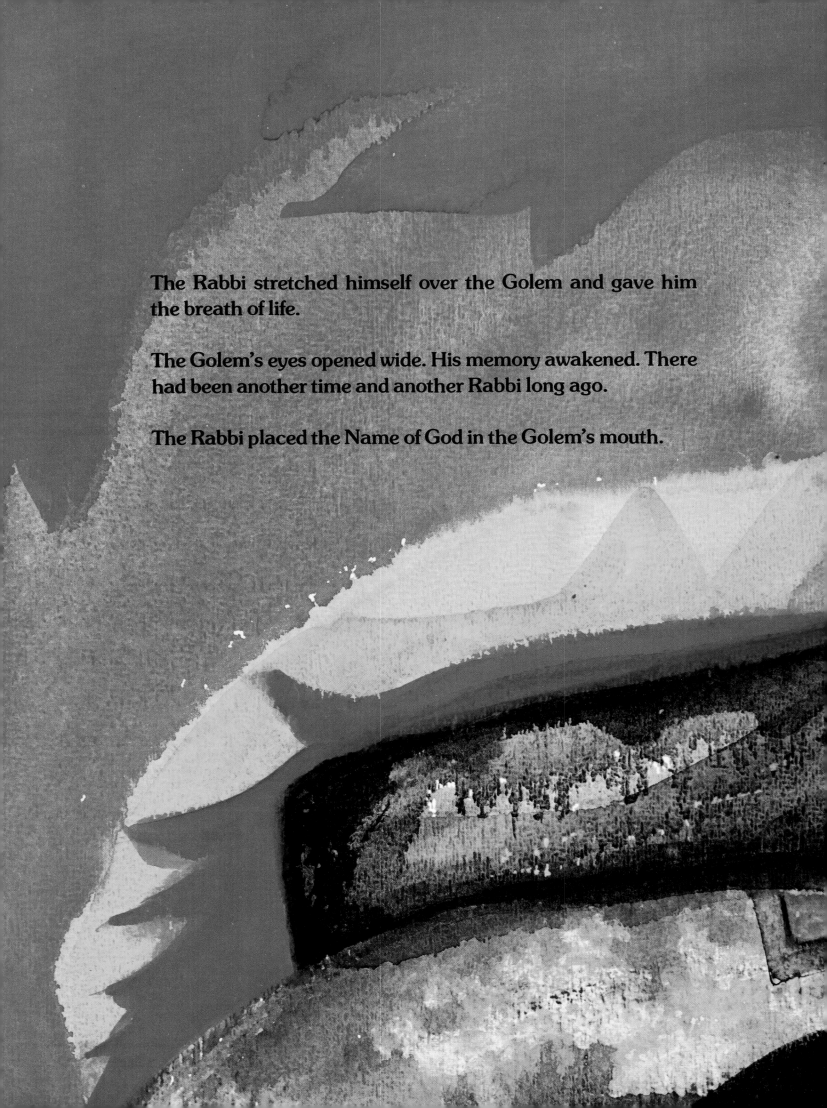

The Rabbi stretched himself over the Golem and gave him the breath of life.

The Golem's eyes opened wide. His memory awakened. There had been another time and another Rabbi long ago.

The Rabbi placed the Name of God in the Golem's mouth.

Daylight flooded the attic and four men descended the narrow stairway.

Rabbi Lev was well satisfied with his work. He thanked God for peace. The Golem would guard the ghetto day and night and warn him of any trouble.

As the days passed, the Golem became a familiar presence everywhere.

He often went to the synagogue and heard the songs of his people.

Every Sabbath he visited each house in the ghetto and lit the hearth fires.

He watched over the preparations for the Seder, the Passover feast that celebrates the time long ago when God helped Moses free the Jews who were slaves in Egypt.

He went out beyond the gates and moved silently among the Gentiles.

On the afternoon of Passover eve, he saw a crowd gathered in the marketplace. A man spoke angrily. "We work our fingers to the bone," he said. "Yet we have nothing to show for it. Our crops rot in the fields. We cannot harvest enough to last the winter."

He pointed toward the ghetto. "There is the cause," he shouted. "The Jews are a plague on our lives! At this very moment they make ready for a feast where they will eat bread made with the blood of our children!"

The Golem watched as the crowd lost their reason. One by one they shouted, "Kill the Jews! Kill the Jews!"

They armed themselves with torches and clubs and headed for the ghetto.

They opened the gates and burned the houses.
The Golem grew into a giant. He raised his arm
and with one powerful blow crushed the angry mob.
The House of Judgment shook and
the light went out of the sky.

The Golem did not stop.

He leveled houses, pulled up trees,

and hurled enormous rocks.

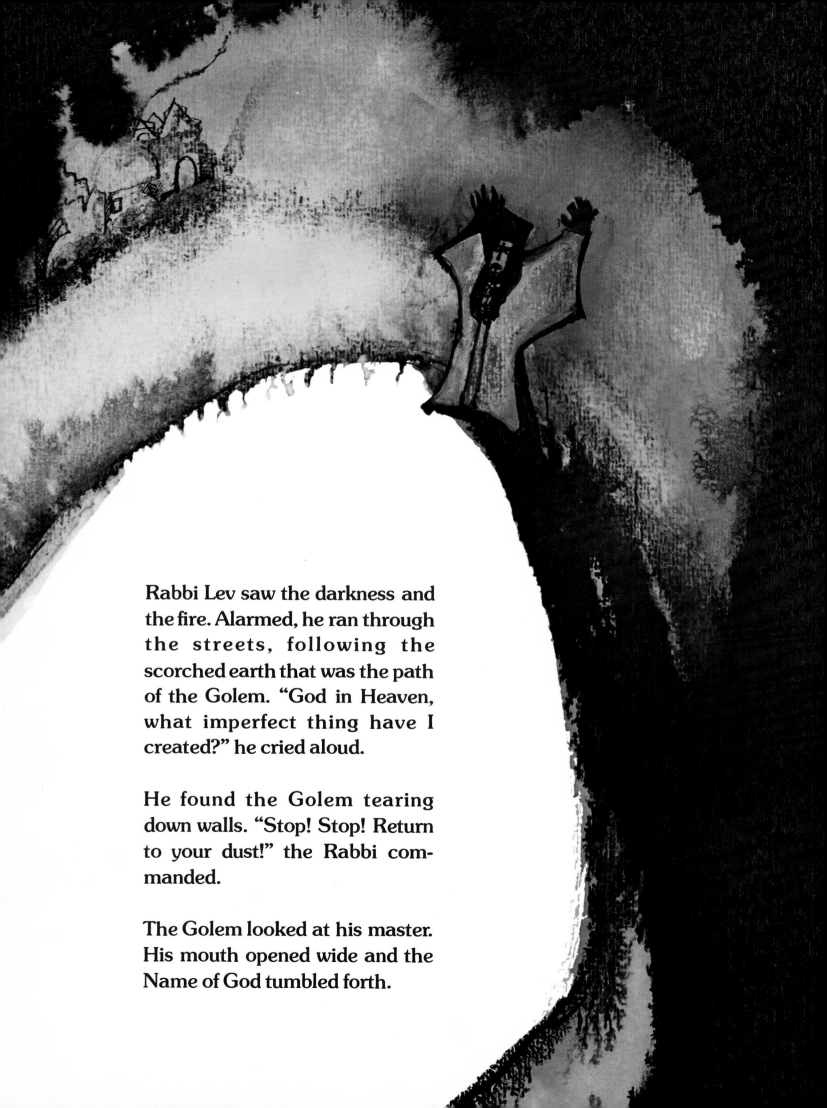

Rabbi Lev saw the darkness and the fire. Alarmed, he ran through the streets, following the scorched earth that was the path of the Golem. "God in Heaven, what imperfect thing have I created?" he cried aloud.

He found the Golem tearing down walls. "Stop! Stop! Return to your dust!" the Rabbi commanded.

The Golem looked at his master. His mouth opened wide and the Name of God tumbled forth.

The Golem crumbled.

Carefully, the Rabbi gathered
up what little remained of the
Golem and looked in sorrow at
the heavens. With a heavy heart
he returned to the synagogue.

Rabbi Lev stood in the darkness of the attic. Deep in thought, he placed the sacred clay once more beneath the holy prayer books.